Rotten Ralph's Rotten Romance

Written by JACK GANTOS *Illustrated by* NICOLE RUBEL

HOUGHTON MIFFLIN COMPANY BOSTON

To Madeline–J.G.

To My Husband–N.R.

Text copyright © 1997 by John B. Gantos, Jr.
Illustrations copyright © 1997 by Nicole Rubel

Library of Congress Cataloging-in-Publication Data

Gantos, Jack.
   Rotten Ralph's rotten romance / by Jack Gantos; illustrated by Nicole Rubel.
      p.cm.
   Summary: It is Valentine's Day, and Rotten Ralph, a very, very nasty cat,
is up to his rotten tricks.
   RNF ISBN: 0-395-73978-0   PAP ISBN: 0-618-49486-3
   [1. Valentine's Day–Fiction. 2 Valentines–Fiction. 3. Cats–Fiction.
4. Behavior–Fiction]   I. Rubel, Nicole, ill.   II. Title.
PZ7.G15534Rokj   1997
[E]–dc20   95-43098
                                                 CIP
                                                  AC

Rotten Ralph was created by Jack Gantos and Nicole Rubel

Printed in the United States of America
WOZ   10   9   8   7   6   5

One morning Sarah woke Ralph up with
a great big kiss.
"Happy Valentine's Day," she said.
Rotten Ralph put his pillow over his head.

"You better be sweet," said Sarah. "We're going to Petunia's valentine party and you know what that means."

"It means sticky, gooey, wet, drippy kisses," Ralph said to himself. He rubbed smelly garbage over his fur. "No one will kiss me now," he thought.

"Don't be so difficult," said Sarah, as
she sprayed him with perfume. "Everyone needs
love and kisses."
She made two big heart-shaped cards.
To My Secret Valentine, she wrote in each one.
I Love You.
She wrote *Love, Sarah* in her card.
When Sarah wasn't looking, Rotten Ralph
squished a stink bug in his.

Sarah put on a special valentine dress.
It was yellow with red and pink hearts.
She dressed Ralph as Cupid. She gave him
little angel wings and put a halo over his head.
Then she gave him a tiny bow and
some love arrows.
"Be careful with those arrows," said Sarah.
"Whoever you shoot will fall in
love with you."

They went outside and picked daisies.
"This is how you tell if someone special loves
you," said Sarah. She plucked off a petal.
"He loves me." She sighed. She plucked
off another. "He loves me not."
Rotten Ralph pulled all the petals off
his flowers. "Not, not, not," he thought.

In the candy shop Sarah filled a big box
with chocolate-covered cherries. "It is
romantic to share candy with your special
valentine," she said, sighing.
Ralph ate the cherries and replaced them
with ants. Then he closed the box.

"Look, Ralph," said Sarah. She pointed
to a pair of lovebirds in a pet store window.
"Aren't they sweet."
Ralph tried to shoot them with his arrow,
but it bounced off the window.
"I'm warning you, Ralph," said Sarah.
"Anything your arrow hits is going to want
to kiss you."

When they arrived at the party, Petunia
gave Ralph a great big smile.
"He's very shy," Sarah said, and dropped
the valentine cards into a big box.
Petunia slipped a sneaky valentine into the box.
"When you pick a card," she said to Ralph,
"you have to kiss whoever wrote it."

Ralph gave Petunia one of his candies.
"No one will love you if you aren't nice,"
Sarah said to Ralph.
Rotten Ralph did not want to be nice. He
broke all the candy hearts in half.

He poked a goldfish with one of his love arrows. It jumped out of the bowl and kissed him.

When it was time to choose the secret
valentines, Sarah was first in line. She reached
into the box. When she opened the card
she was upset.
"That's not very nice," she cried. "My
secret valentine is a big stink bug."

Petunia picked next. She chose the valentine
with Ralph's picture on it. It
was signed, *To Petunia, Your Sweetheart, Ralph.*
"Kiss me," she said to Ralph.
"She cheated," Ralph thought. "She made that card
herself." He threw all his love arrows
across the room.
"Oh no," cried Sarah.

Suddenly everyone wanted to kiss Ralph.
"Don't kiss me! Don't kiss me!" he said.
But they kissed his nose and ears. They
kissed his whiskers. They tickled his belly.
They called him cutey pie and pretty kitty
and lovebug.
Rotten Ralph groaned. He wanted to go home.

"Before we leave you must kiss Petunia goodbye," said Sarah.
But Petunia refused to kiss Ralph. He had rubbed dog food on his lips.

When they returned home, Sarah filled the
bathtub. She made Ralph take a bath.
"You hurt Petunia's feelings," she said.
"But she's not my valentine," Ralph thought
to himself.

When he was dry he jumped onto Sarah's lap.
"Oh, Ralph," said Sarah, and she fed him a chocolate
kiss. "You are my favorite valentine."
"I am wonderful," thought Ralph.
Then Sarah gave him a valentine kiss.